Teach Trade!

By Jennie Warmouth & Gabriel Ayerza

Illustrated by Aya T. Sato

For Miss Wright
~J.W.

Acknowledgements

A very special thanks to **The U.S. Department of State Fulbright Program** for sponsoring Jennie M. Warmouth's International Teacher Exchange to Scotland (2008-09), her return visit to Scotland (2011), and for funding the publication of this book (2012).

With love and thanks to: Mummy & Daddy Warmouth, Stefanie Warmouth, Heather Inglis, Hilda Inglis, Susan Imrie, Kirsten Wright, Anna Walter, Mary Duff, Kirsty Campbell, Kristen Timmons, the darling Primary 2 class, and Dr. Brinda Jegatheesan.

Dear Readers,

My name is Jennie and I am a first and second grade teacher in Seattle, Washington. One year I traded classrooms with a teacher named Heather in SCOTLAND! I moved to Scotland and she moved to America. I lived in her *flat* and she lived in my *apartment*. I taught her Scottish *pupils* and she taught my American *students*. We had lots of fun but were surprised to discover all of the differences between American English and Scottish English. Sometimes the words *sounded* the same but meant something different and sometimes the same things had *different names* all together!

Heather & Jennie

It was confusing! Luckily, our brilliant students came to the rescue time and time again! We hope you enjoy reading both sides of our silly story!

 Jennie

Twice upon a time, two teachers traded lives.
This story begins as the *other* arrives.

Miss Cue landed in Scotland, where a cow is a *coo*.
"Teaching will be easy," she thought. "Scots speak English too!"

She jumped in a taxi, all black and not yellow,
but it took all her focus to understand the ol' fellow!

They zipped past the castle on the left side of the road.
The driver spoke quickly in a heavy Scottish brogue.

When they got to the school, he said, "Yer bag's in the boot."
She looked at his feet and said, "You're silly and cute!"

"Yer twenty-five pounds, miss?" he requested then hollered.
"I'm one-ten," she quipped and tipped him a dollar.

The head teacher told her, "Your room is just there.
Simply follow your pupils round there past the stair."

The children so darling all sat in their places.
Miss Cue set to learning their names and sweet faces.

"I'm very glad to be here to teach you this year!
I'll try to speak slowly so my directions are clear."

"Let's start out with spelling—so easy you'll pass!
Please take out your notebooks and erasers dear class."

Unsure what she meant but polite nonetheless,
Amy whispered, "Jotters and rubbers?" to the rest.

With careful dictation, Miss Cue read down the list
but was terribly alarmed by the words they all missed.

"May I wash in the toilet?" Thomas asked with a twinkle.
"Heavens, no!" Miss Cue squealed. "Toilets are only for tinkle!"

He didn't need the bathroom! Where was his potty dance?
Miss Cue told Thomas to wipe his hands on his **pants!**

Thomas looked shocked! The class burst into laughter.
Students fell to the floor. Cameron swung from the rafters!

In stormed the custodian, "That's no way to behave!
This here is a CLASSROOM! Not a swing park or cave!"

Exhausted and confused, Miss Cue needed lunch soon,
but the kids said that *dinner* is the meal served at noon.

Listening for the special, she heard "mints pie."
Her favorite herb in a pastry? Now there's one to try!

She took her first bite, expecting refreshing and sweet,
but instead tasted savory and realized it was BEEF!

She went back and asked for some biscuits instead
but was handed some cookies rather than bread.

"These are cookies not biscuits and my pie contains meat!
With all of these mix-ups, how do you eat???"

Fed up, Freddy stood up. Enough was enough!
Miss Cue must learn Scottish or her time would be tough.

"That music you hear? It comes from a *piper*!
Those babies you smell wear *nappies* not diapers!"

"The trunk is the boot, while a boot is a welly.
A wallet's a purse and a TV's a telly!"

"Now really, Miss Cue! Enough of this blether!
It's time you learn Scottish. We'll do it together!"

They nipped back to class and the learning began.
The kids worked together like a wee Scottish clan.

One at a time, they imparted their knowledge.
Miss Cue took notes as if it were college.

"A mom is a *mum* and a grandma's a *granny*.
A dad's still a dad but an *au pair's* a nanny."

"You live in a *flat* and the yard is the *garden*.
It's rude to ask, 'what?'; more polite to ask '*pardon?*'"

"Your *pants* go under your trousers and vest.
A *jumper's* the woolly you wear on your chest!"

"It isn't a line but rather a *queue*.
The toilet's the toilet, yet the bathroom's the *loo*!"

And so teacher and student each traded turns.
The story continues as the *other* one learns.

Twice upon a time, two teachers traded lives.
This story begins as the *other* arrives.

Miss Queue landed in America, a nation so new!
"Teaching will be easy," she thought. "Yanks speak English too!"

Seattle was lovely but the distances quite far.
Miss Queue claimed her cases and waved for a car.

"To the school, not my flat," she told the driver she hired
then wondered to herself why he spoke of burst tyres.

Stores flashed with bright colours! The motorway was uncanny!
Loads of shoppes had car tunnels! Buildings were younger than grannies!

"Twenty bucks!" the driver said, a price ten times two deer.
Thinking him daft, she paid cash and said, "Cheers!"

Hurdling her luggage, the kids budged for an embrace.
"You're lovely," Miss Queue beamed, "but get off my case."

The principal told her, "Follow the path to the bend.
Cross three courtyards and nine buildings—you'll be in Room Ten."

The lessons went nicely, and Miss Queue was right pleased
until "show-and-tell" brought parents, pets and babies!

"Is it Boxing Day?" Miss Queue asked, "Or is this some kind of show?"
"There's no punching!" said Sue. "We just get in a row!"

Miss Queue said to a wee baby, "Your dummy's cute too!"
Then saw a puppy in a party dress and asked, "Do doggies do dos?"

When the parrot took off, Miss Queue shrieked, "Mind the loose bird!"
The good students flapped about, following the teacher to her word.

Miss Queue squawked, "Caw canny!" and the parrot repeated.
When the bird took to his perch, the kids gladly reseated.

John let loose a yawn and asked for a nappy.
The thought of him skipping the loo made Miss Queue quite unhappy!

Politely she said, "This school hasn't a shower.
Please go to the **toilet** before messing your trousers."

Sleepy John looked gutted—then the principal called.
Miss Queue's class was late! Lunch service was stalled!

"Chop, chop!" Miss Queue urged. "Now chivvy along!"
They hurried to lunch but the food seemed all wrong.

14

Hamburger on her tray, Miss Queue asked for some chips.
Strangely, however, she was given some crisps.

She was offered some eggplant—though eggs come from chickens!
Then a plate full of hush puppies? Thinking of shoes made her sicken!

Desperate for a sweetie, she asked for some chocs.
But that cheeky dinner lady served a stationery box!

"These are crisps, not chips! I'd like a confection, not chalk!
With all of these mix-ups, how do you talk???"

Bravely, Gracie spoke up! Enough was enough!
Miss Queue needed help or her time would be tough.

"Cheerios are breakfast—not a way to say 'bye'!
We like to say *yes, sure, yeah*, but not *aye*!"

"We say *boy* not mate, and *girl* not lass.
It's a *toot* not a pump when you pass a li'l gas."

"Dear Miss Queue, this silliness must end.
We're all here to help you. We want to be friends!"

Back in the classroom, the kids took the lead.
They would teach Miss Queue all that she'd need.

"It's not a full stop, but a *period*; not a zed, but a *zee*.
We say *like* instead of fancy and *little* instead of wee!"

"Our *baby teeth* are your milk teeth. Your wobbly's our *loose*.
We prefer to say *soda* for your fizzy juice!"

"It's *soccer* not footie, and a *cleat* not a boot.
It's *recess* not break time, and a *slide* not a chute."

"It's *pacifier* not dummy, and *party* not do.
Please just say *bathroom*—not toilet or loo!"

"We like what is *awesome* while you're keen on what's ace.
Here a person is called brilliant—not a thing or a place!"

And so teacher and student each traded turns.
The story continues as the *other* one learns.

About the Authors

Jennie Warmouth is a teacher and a Ph.D. candidate researching Human Development & Cognition at the University of Washington.

Gabriel Ayerza has an MFA in Creative Writing, authors weekly haikus and is currently completing his first novel.

Aya T. Sato is a photographer and visual artist in Seattle, WA.

Please visit us online at www.teacher-trade.com

CPSIA information can be obtained
at www.ICGtesting.com
Printed in the USA
LVIC01n1642291113
363225LV00002B/40

9 781479 210459